STONE AGE!

WELCOME TO THE STONE AGE . . . AND THE WORLD OF THE CAVEMICE!

CAPITAL: OLD MOUSE CITY

POPULATION: WE'RE NOT SURE. (MATH DOESN'T EXIST YET!) BUT BESIDES CAVEMICE, THERE ARE PLENTY OF DINOSAURS, <u>WAY</u> TOO MANY SABER-TOOTHED TIGERS, AND FEROCIOUS CAVE BEARS — BUT NO MOUSE HAS EVER HAD THE COURAGE TO COUNT THEM!

TYPICAL FOOD: PETRIFIED CHEESE SOUP

NATIONAL HOLIDAY: **GREAT ZAP DAY**, WHICH CELEBRATES THE DISCOVERY OF FIRE. RODENTS EXCHANGE GRILLED CHEESE SANDWICHES ON THIS HOLIDAY.

NATIONAL DRINK: MAMMOTH MILKSHAKES

CLIMATE: Unpredictable, WITH FREQUENT METEOR SHOWERS

cheese soup

milkshake

MONEY

SEASHELLS OF ALL SHAPES AND SIZES

MEASUREMENT

THE BASIC UNIT OF MEASUREMENT IS BASED ON THE LENGTH OF THE TAIL OF THE LEADER OF THE VILLAGE. A UNIT CAN BE DIVIDED INTO A HALF TAIL OR QUARTER TAIL. THE LEADER IS ALWAYS READY TO PRESENT HIS TAIL WHEN THERE IS A DISPUTE.

THE CAVEMICE

Geronimo

Trap

Thea

Benjamin

Bugsy Wugsy

Hercule Poirat

Grandma Ratrock

Geronimo Stilton

CAVEMICE

GET THE SCOOP, GERONIMO!

Scholastic Inc.

Copyright © 2012 by Edizioni Piemme S.p.A., Palazzo Mondadori, Via Mondadori 1, 20090 Segrate, Italy. International Rights © Atlantyca S.p.A. English translation © 2015 by Atlantyca S.p.A.

The publisher does not have any control over and does not assume any responsibility for author or third-party websites or their content.

GERONIMO STILTON names, characters, and related indicia are copyright, trademark, and exclusive license of Atlantyca S.p.A. All rights reserved. The moral right of the author has been asserted. Based on an original idea by Elisabetta Dami. www.geronimostilton.com

Published by Scholastic Inc., 557 Broadway, New York, NY 10012. SCHOLASTIC and associated logos are trademarks and/or registered trademarks of Scholastic Inc.

Stilton is the name of a famous English cheese. It is a registered trademark of the Stilton Cheese Makers' Association. For more information, go to www.stiltoncheese.com.

No part of this publication may be reproduced, stored in a retrieval system, or transmitted in any form or by any means, electronic, mechanical, photocopying, recording, or otherwise, without written permission of the copyright holder. For information regarding permission, please contact: Atlantyca S.p.A., Via Leopardi 8, 20123 Milan, Italy; e-mail foreignrights@atlantyca.it, www.atlantyca.com.

This book is a work of fiction. Names, characters, places, and incidents are either the product of the author's imagination or are used fictitiously, and any resemblance to actual persons, living or dead, business establishments, events, or locales is entirely coincidental.

ISBN 978-0-545-83550-3

Text by Geronimo Stilton
Original title *Cadono notizie da urlo, Stiltonùt!*
Cover by Flavio Ferron
Illustrations by Giuseppe Facciotto (design) and Alessandro Costa (color)
Graphics by Marta Lorini and Chiara Cebraro

Special thanks to Tracey West
Translated by Lidia Morson Tramontozzi
Interior design by Becky James

10 9 8 7 6 5 4 3 2 1   15 16 17 18 19

Printed in the U.S.A.   40
First printing 2015

MANY AGES AGO, ON PREHISTORIC MOUSE ISLAND, THERE WAS A VILLAGE CALLED OLD MOUSE CITY. IT WAS INHABITED BY BRAVE *RODENT SAPIENS* KNOWN AS THE CAVEMICE. DANGERS SURROUNDED THE MICE AT EVERY TURN: EARTHQUAKES, METEOR SHOWERS, FEROCIOUS DINOSAURS, AND FIERCE GANGS OF SABER-TOOTHED TIGERS. BUT THE BRAVE CAVEMICE FACED IT ALL WITH A SENSE OF HUMOR, AND WERE ALWAYS READY TO LEND A HAND TO OTHERS.

HOW DO I KNOW THIS? I DISCOVERED AN ANCIENT BOOK WRITTEN BY MY ANCESTOR, GERONIMO STILTONOOT! HE CARVED HIS STORIES INTO STONE TABLETS AND ILLUSTRATED THEM WITH HIS ETCHINGS.

I AM PROUD TO SHARE THESE STONE AGE STORIES WITH YOU. THE EXCITING ADVENTURES OF THE CAVEMICE WILL MAKE YOUR FUR STAND ON END, AND THE JOKES WILL TICKLE YOUR WHISKERS! HAPPY READING!

Geronimo Stilton

WARNING! DON'T IMITATE THE CAVEMICE. WE'RE NOT IN THE STONE AGE ANYMORE!

CRAAASH!

It was a quiet morning in late summer. The sun hung like a wheel of cheddar in the sky. The clouds played catch with one another, and the flags swayed gently in the chilly breeze in the harbor of Old Mouse City. The village was buzzing with excitement about the **RODENT RAFT RACE**, a thrilling Stone Age rafting competition.

I, **GERONIMO STILTONOOT**, was especially excited. I am the publisher of *The Stone Gazette*, the most famouse newspaper in the Stone Age (probably because it's the only one!), and I was planning a **SPECIAL EDITION** about the race.

It was almost time for the rafts to shove off. I was hanging around the pier looking for a scoop with my assistant, WILEY UPSNOOT.

"Boss! Look!" he cried.

"Shh, Wiley, I'm busy!" I snapped. "And please don't call me **boss**. Okay?"

"Okay, boss, sure," Wiley said. "But it looks like the weather is **changing**. Look over there!"

"We're not here to watch the **weather**," I said. "We're here to wor —"

I'm busy!

But . . .

PETRIFIED CHEESE!

I suddenly noticed that Wiley was right! The sky had become dark — very dark. The big, fat clouds weren't playing nicely anymore. They were moving fast — very fast. A **WIND** of megalithic proportions was sweeping over the sea.

The waves began to churn, and they rose up tall — very tall. Then the giant waves charged right toward the pier!

TRUMPETING TRICERATOPS! I HAD NEVER SEEN ANYTHING LIKE IT!

We cavemice are used to disasters. Every day, we face ERUPTING volcanoes, **powerful** earthquakes, and **meteor** showers. As a matter of fact, we don't ever leave our **CAVES** without making a will. That's just what life is like in the Stone Age!

But the rodents on the pier were too excited to notice the storm. **Ernest Heftymouse**, the leader of our village, got ready to start the race.

He walked to the gong used to start important events. I began to panic. I had to warn him! I waved my stone tablet in the air.

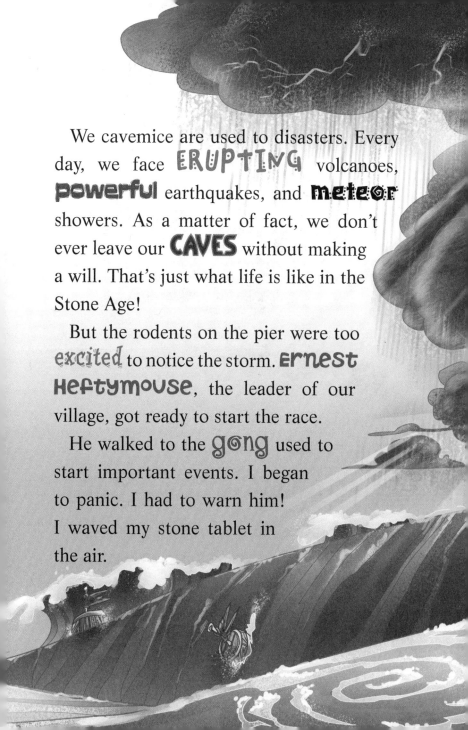

Let the race begin!

WHOOOOOSH!

A gust of wind swept across the bleachers. My stone tablet flew from my paws.

CRAAAAASH!

Ernest looked at me, annoyed.

I called to him. "Sorry, I just wanted to tell you that —"

WHOOOOOOOOOOSH!

A gust of wind, much stronger than the first, ripped the club from Ernest's paw. It flew up, up, up, and . . .

BONK!

. . . landed on my skull! Ouch! What a Paleolithic pain! Then . . .

WHOOOooooooOSH!

The wind knocked me over! I **toppled** off the pier and fell headfirst into one of the rafts.

I sighed with relief. (Squeak! At least I didn't end up in the water!) But that was the end of my good luck.

BAM! A wave hit the raft, sending me and the crew SPLASHiNG into the water.

"Cavemice overboard!" yelled Ernest.

The **FIRST AID** team jumped in to save us. Ernest Heftymouse must have finally noticed the storm, because he announced, "A storm is coming! The Rodent Raft Race is postponed!

RUN FOR YOUR LIVES!"

THE STONE AGE RATITZER AWARD

I had just stepped onto the pier, when . . .

Plunk! plunk! Plunk!

Rotten ricotta! As if we needed **RAIN**! My fur was already soaked, and I didn't want to catch a cold. I darted under the shelter of a small lean-to with some other rodents who had taken cover from the rain. We crowded together and it was a tight fit — a very **TIGHT** fit. I had one rodent's knee in my ear, an **elbow** in my face, and a tail tapping my head. I even had whiskers in my eye!

The conditions were tough, but I had to

keep working. I took out my spare STONE TABLET. I began to CHISEL a story about the race being postponed. I lifted my hammer and . . . BANG! Instead of hitting the tablet, I hit the knee of the rodent next to me.

"OUCH! Watch out, will you?"

"Oops! Sorry," I said.

I started chiseling again. BONK! I

Hey!

Ouch!

accidentally hit someone's tail.

"**YIKES!** What's the matter with you?"

"Really sorry," I said.

"That's it!" someone yelled. "Out of here, you troublesome cavemouse!"

"Out! Out! Out!" the others chanted.

They pushed me out and . . .

SPLASH!

I landed in a puddle of mud!

Then a screeching voice filled the air.

"MEGA-EXTRA-SPECIAL NEWS FLASH!"

It was Sally Rockmousen. She runs Gossip Radio, the most inaccurate, dishonest, and just plain fake news station in the Stone Age.

"Hear all about it! **Clumsy Geronimo Stiltonoot** causes cancellation of Rodent Raft Race!"

13

"What?" I exclaimed. That wasn't true at all! It was not **MY fault** that the Rodent Raft Race was canceled. It was because of the terrible **storm** and the churning **waves**!

But sadly, that is how Gossip Radio works. Sally squeaks the news out loud, and it gets passed on by other rodents and **SHRIEKERS**, loud-beaked prehistoric birds. Someone will **SHOUT** it out, and then the next rodent or shrieker will REPEAT what he hears, and so will the next. By the time it gets to the last rodent, the news doesn't make any SENSE!

I tried to find Wiley (where had he gone?) when I heard my friend Hercule Poirat's voice.

"Geronimo! Are you okay?" he asked.

"Actually, not real —"

"Yes, I heard!" Hercule interrupted me.

14

"Those shriekers are piercing my eardrums."

I frowned. "Sally doesn't seem to care what she makes up so long as she wins the **STONE AGE RATITZER AWARD**."

"What's the Ratitzer?" Hercule asked.

"Don't you know? It's the AWARD for the best prehistoric news reporting," I told him.

Flood warning!

Blood warming!

Mud storming!

Hercule nodded. "There's no way that Sally can win that. She only reports fake news!"

"I agree," I said, and then sighed. "But her fake news gets everyone's attention. I am afraid that Ernest Heftymouse will present the award to her tonight. I need to break a **BIG STORY** if *The Stone Gazette* is going to win."

We headed back to the news office. To warm us up, I fixed us two cups of steamy hot cheese, the favorite drink of chilly cavemice.

Ah, how cheesily delicious!

The warm drink was exactly what I nee —

WHOOOOOOOSH!

Before I could take a sip, the door BURST open. In came a gust of rain along with my sister, Thea. She was riding her autosaurus, a velociraptor named Grunty.

"GERONIMO! WE'RE IN BIG TROUBLE!"

AAACHOOO!

"What do you mean, **THEA**?" I asked as I tried to make myself smaller and smaller and smaller. Before she could answer, Grunty exploded in a deafening sneeze that sprayed my whole face.

"AAH . . . AAH . . . AAACHOOO!"

ACHOO!

Oh!

YUCK!

"We need to find a **big news scoop**, fast!" Thea exclaimed. "We can't let Sally win the Stone Age Ratitzer Award!"

Truthfully, I didn't really **care** if we won the award. It was more important to me to do a good job as a reporter. I always check all of my **FACTS** carefully! But for Thea, winning the Ratitzer was a big deal.

"Sally is a fake!" she scoffed. "She's as **SLIPPERY** as melted cheese. She doesn't care about the truth at all."

"You're right!" exclaimed Wiley, looking out from behind a stack of STONE TABLETS.

She's a fake!

"Wiley? Where have you been?" I asked.

"I was right in front of

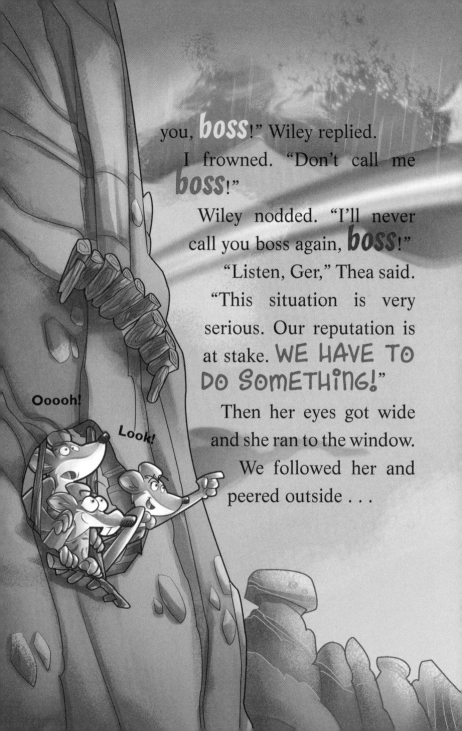

you, **boss**!" Wiley replied.

I frowned. "Don't call me **boss**!"

Wiley nodded. "I'll never call you boss again, **boss**!"

"Listen, Ger," Thea said. "This situation is very serious. Our reputation is at stake. WE HAVE TO DO SOMETHING!"

Then her eyes got wide and she ran to the window.

We followed her and peered outside . . .

Ooooh!

Look!

"Oooooooooooh!"

"Mousetastic!" cried Hercule.

A beautiful rainbow stretched across the sky.

It was a truly spectacular sight!

Just then we heard Sally's voice screeching through the city. Her squeak was as irritating as a pterodactyl with a sore throat.

"NEWS FLASH! THE BASE OF THE RAINBOW HAS BEEN DISCOVERED IN OLD MOUSE CITY!"

Thea, Hercule, and I exchanged an amazed look.

THE BASE OF THE RAINBOW ... DISCOVERED? HOW WAS THAT POSSIBLE?

"Fascinating! Let's go see it," said Hercule.

"Wiley, stay here and get the tablets ready," I said. "We'll be right back with —"

"A whisker-licking-good **scoop**!" Thea finished for me.

We took off like a bolt of LIGHTNING, searching for the base of the rainbow. Grunty followed us, sneezing all the way.

Moldy mozzarella!

My fur was getting soaked.

"Grunty, if you don't stop sneezing on me, I'll flatten you like a grilled cheese sandwich!" I told him.

SCOOP OR FLOP?

We *RACED* through the village, but we didn't see the base of the rainbow — or a single mouse.

GREAT ROCKY BOULDERS! WHERE WAS EVERYBODY?

It was very odd. We made our way to the park in the center of Old Mouse City. There we found Ernest Heftymouse arguing with **Sally Rockmousen** in the middle of a massive crowd of rodents. Sally's shrill squeak rose above all the others.

Sally's shrieks can **SHATTER** granite! I put my paws over my ears, but I heard her anyway.

Sally Rockmousen

First Name: Sally

Last Name: Rockmousen

Favorite Color: Putrid pink

Personality: Loud

Favorite Expression: "News flash!"

Profession: Host of Gossip Radio, the fakest news source in Old Mouse City

Hobby: Plotting against her good-natured rival, Geronimo Stiltonoot!

"Here we are!" announced Sally. She pointed to three nervous-looking cavemice behind her. "According to my witnesses, the rainbow was resting right on this stone. When the rainbow vanished, its **COLORS** remained on the rock. You can see it with your own eyes!"

"Oooooooooooooooooh!"

Everyone was squeakless. Sally appeared to be telling the truth.

The huge slab of stone in front of Sally was smeared with **COLORS**. In fact, the colors looked wet. Thea, Hercule, and I looked at one another. We were all thinking the same thing: HOW STRANGE!

Ernest questioned the three witnesses. "So you all saw the rainbow leave its **COLORS** on this rock?" he asked.

They didn't reply, and I noticed them hiding their paws behind their backs.

HOW VERY STRANGE!

Then Sally nudged them, and the three mice spoke up.

"Uh, yep, we were here!"

"Yeah, right here!"

"We were here, there, and over there!"

HOW VERY, VERY STRANGE!

Sally's goons didn't convince me one bit! They easily could have *smeared* the slab with their own paws. But how could I prove it?

"Are you lying so that Sally will win?" Thea asked them. "COME ON! TELL THE TRUTH!"

"Don't listen to her!" Sally shouted

angrily. "Thea, you're just jealous of the ＳｕＣＣｅＳＳ of Gossip Radio!"

Before Thea could protest, Ernest chimed in.

"Sally may be right. *The Stone Gazette* hasn't had any big stories lately," he said. "And with this kind of news, Gossip Radio

is a whisker away from winning the **STONE AGE RATITZER**!"

Sally laughed. "Ha! Did you hear that, you SLAB chiselers? You're doomed!"

The crowd of rodents cheered and applauded loudly. Sally smiled a WICKED smile.

"Bouncing bananas, she's such a show-off!" Hercule said. "But we'll show her. Isn't that right, Geronimo?"

I nodded. Before, I hadn't cared about winning the Ratitzer. But now I *had* to win. My pride was on the line.

FOSSILIZED FETA, SALLY WAS NOT GOING TO GET AWAY WITH THIS!

HUNTING FOR A SCOOP

Deep in thought, we returned to *The Stone Gazette*'s headquarters. Hercule was furious.

"That Sally is not a journalist. She's a fraud!" he cried.

"YOU'RE RIGHT! AND WE WILL GET TO THE BOTTOM OF HER DECEPTION!" cried Thea.

The thought of going after Sally made my whiskers quake. I have seen her when she's angry. She could crush me like a brontosaurus stepping on a bug!

"Um, maybe going after Sally isn't the best plan," I said.

"What? Are you just giving up?"

Thea asked angrily.

"No!" I said. "I mean, maybe we just need to find a good story. A good, HONEST story."

Thea nodded. "Of course! That's exactly what we need to do. We'll find a terrific news story, and then that big phony Sally won't win the Ratitzer."

"Um, but how can we find a big story so

Are you giving up?

Um, no!

soon?" I asked. "It's not like one will just FALL out of the sky."

"Unless there's a **meteor shower**," Hercule piped up.

"Think positive, Geronimo!" Thea demanded. She SLAPPED me on the back with the force of a boulder. (Boy, she really wanted to win!) "You and I are Stiltonoots. We have a **nose** for news. So let's get out there and start **sniffing**!"

When Thea sets her mind to something, there is no way to stop her. And Hercule was just as determined. So when Thea scampered out onto the street with Hercule at her heels, I knew I had to follow them.

"Where should we **sniff** first?" Hercule asked. "Old Mouse City is a big place. News could be hiding anywhere."

"Hmm," Thea said, and then her eyes lit up. "I know. Let's go to the ROTTEN TOOTH TAVERN! Maybe our cousin Trap has something delicious to tell us."

"Good idea," Hercule agreed.

"This is a great plan," said Thea as we walked. "As Geronimo said, we can't expect news to fall from the sky."

SPLAT!

A ripe tomato hit me right in the face!

Not far from Trap's tavern, a small crowd of rodents was tossing every kind of vegetable at a very short, very fat, well-dressed rodent.

"That's **Rocco Caruso**, the famous opera singer!" said Thea.

Thea didn't have to tell me who he was. Rocco is known by every rodent in the Stone Age! His powerful VOICE is loved throughout the prehistoric world. But something was wrong. The crowd was angry, and Rocco was standing on the stage, looking SAD — very SAD. And he was as **quiet** as a mouse.

"What happened?" Hercule asked.

A mouse with a pawful of rotten cabbage answered him.

"What happened is that Rocco can't seem to sing! As soon as he opens his mouth, only squeaks and whistles come out!"

"SHAME ON YOU! WE PAID FIFTY SEASHELLS TO HEAR YOU!"

yelled a rodent as he hurled a **ROTTEN** eggplant at the poor opera singer.

Rocco looked so **embarrassed**! He cleared his throat and tried to sing his song once more.

La-la-la-eeeeeeek!

"I love you more than ma-ma-ma-mozzarella! Please let me be your special fa-fa-fa-fella!"

He got the words out this time, but his voice was awful. He sounded like a brontosaurus with a **bad cold**!

"This could be the big news story we need," Thea whispered to me, but right then we heard . . .

"NEWS FLASH!"

It was Sally, screaming like a pterodactyl from the top of Gossip Radio's rock.

"The famouse opera singer Rocco Caruso has lost his voice! There's a *huge reward* for the rodent who finds it!"

How could this happen? I couldn't believe it. That big fake Sally had snatched our fabumouse piece of news right out of our paws!

GRANDMA'S CURE

"Bones and stones!" I cried. "That's just not fair."

Thea looked thoughtful. "Hmm. I have an idea. Follow me!"

We DUCKED flying vegetables as my sister led us up to the stage. Rocco had climbed down and was hiding behind it, trying to clean his FUR. He looked so miserable.

Thea approached him, her big VIOLET EYES full of sympathy.

"Maestro Caruso, we are big admirers of yours," she began. "We are so sorry about your voice. We would love to cheer you up. Will you join us for dinner?"

SURPRISED, the opera singer cracked a smile.

"I do feel a little hungry . . . *Eek!*" he replied.

At least, that's what I think he said. His voice was CRACKING and squeaking terribly, and he was difficult to understand.

"WHAT DID HE SAY? THAT HE'S HUNGRY?"

Hercule asked. "It's too bad he got pelted by rotten veggies. At least the angry crowd could have thrown some double-cheese PIZZAS, or barbecued ribs, or **cheese balls**, or something."

"**EEK!** I will gladly accept your invitation," Rocco said as he rubbed his belly. "Well then, la-la-la-let's go to da-da-da-dinner!"

Hercule nudged me. "What's he saying? I can't Understand a word."

"Shhh!" Thea warned. "Rocco is very TOUCHY. He said he'll join us for dinner, and that's exactly what we need for my plan to work."

Hercule and I both nodded. I was very curious to see what Thea had in mind.

We led him to the Rotten Tooth Tavern and found a table inside. My cousin Trap brought us a MENU, and Rocco licked his lips as he looked at it.

"La-la-la-let's see!" he said. "I would like a dish of grilled peppers with blue cheese sauce, twenty pterodactyl eggs — why don't we make it twenty-one? An extra is always better. And a platter of Jurassic cheese balls, and a salad with cheese croutons."

"What? No dessert?" asked Hercule sarcastically.

"Of course! Dessert!" Rocco said.

He eyed the menu once more. "La-la-la-let's end this delicious meal with two strawberry **Cheesecakes** and some **cheese cookies**! Yes, that should da-da-da-do it!"

"Are you sure that's enough?" Hercule asked.

"Not really. This a very la-la-la-light dinner!" Rocco said. Right away he began chowing down.

Chomp, chomp, chomp!

Rocco devoured the food like a SABER-TOOTHED TIGER tearing apart prey and finished it all in record time. After he was done, I saw Thea whisper something in Trap's ear. He scampered into the kitchen and returned with three mugs of steaming liquid.

"This is our house specialty stomach settler!" he announced.

Hercule and I tasted it first.

"Yum," I said as it slid down my throat. The brew was very warm, very sweet, and . . .

VEEEEEEEERY SPICY!

My mouth was on **FIRE**! My face turned **bright red**. I ran between the tables until I found a pitcher of **ICY** water and dunked my snout right in it. Hercule ran out of the tavern like a **lightning bolt** and dove off the pier into the water!

But Rocco seemed to like the drink. Thea was grinning from ear to ear.

"Why are you so **happy**?" I asked her.

"Hee, hee! You mean

SHAMAN
BEE

you didn't recognize the drink?" my sister asked.

Then it hit me. "That wasn't Trap's stomach settler. That was Grandma Ratrock's cure for a sore throat!"

Thea nodded. "Right! It's her special recipe: scalding water from the gurgling geyser, a pawful of Paleozoic hot pepper, and a spoonful of honey from the famous shaman bees."

"What? SHAMAN BEES?" asked Hercule, returning to the dining room with soaked fur.

"They are rare bees that make honey with great HEALING properties," Thea explained.

"The honey is very spicy, but it is strong

enough to heal the sore throat of a **T. REX**," I added.

Thea grinned again. "If it cures Rocco, then he will be able to sing again. And we'll have the **scoop** before Sally does!"

Rocco drank every last drop of Grandma's cure. Then he set down his mug and let out a burp that made the walls of the tavern tremble.

BUUUUUUUUUUUURP!

"What a ba-ba-ba-burp!" he sang out, and I gasped. His wonderful, deep operatic VOICE was back!

"Excellent!" said Rocco. "Now I can sa-sa-sa-sing!"

He began to sing out perfect scales.

♪ ♪ **"DO RE MI FA SOL ♪ LA TI DO!"** ♪ ♪

Thea quickly began to chisel out a story about Rocco's miraculous recovery. This time, we were going to beat out Gossip Radio for sure!

Rocco kept singing his scales, and the guests at the tavern applauded **loudly**. Then he burst into song again. This time, he hit a very, very **high note** at the end.

♪ "I LOVE YOU MORE THAN BA-BA-BA-BLUE CHEEEEEEEEESE!" ♪

The note was so high that every cup and plate in the tavern shattered . . . along with the stone slab that Thea was chiseling! Oh no! Our special edition was now in a **THOUSAND PIECES**!

"There goes our scoop." Thea sighed.

"Let's hurry back to the office and CHISEL another one!" I said.

While Rocco kept singing, we raced from the tavern as fast as a HURTLING meteorite. But right as we got to the office, Sally's voice was already screeching:

"**NEWS FLASH!** Rocco Caruso finds his voice. Or did his voice find Rocco? Details in our next report."

STOP! DON'T YOU DARE!

Great rocky boulders! **Sally** had beaten us again! Things were looking very bad.

We stopped racing and caught our breath. We picked up some more TABLETS and then wandered away slowly. Thea helped Grunty blow his nose, and Hercule and I decided to take a rest under a palm tree. We were about to sit down when —

"STOP! DON'T YOU DARE!"

The voice belonged to Professor Frank Flowerfur, the most famous botanist in Old Mouse City. He shook his head at us.

"Why does nobody pay attention to the

beauty that is right at their feet?" he grumbled. "You two were about to sit on the very rare hardrock rose!"

Stunning!

FRANK FLOWERFUR

I looked down and saw some blue-gray roses poking up from the grass. They looked sort of shriveled.

Frank bent over them. "Danger averted, my dear little roses."

"What makes these dried-up flowers so special?" Hercule asked.

Suddenly, a flower bent over and smashed Hercule's foot!

"*Ouuuuuuuch!*"

"It serves you right," said Frank. "Hardrock roses have very hard petals and their feelings get hurt easily, so be careful what you say!"

That got Thea's attention. "These are very special flowers."

"That is true!" said Frank. "Hardrock roses normally grow only in the **Stinky Swamp**, the habitat of the saber-toothed tigers. It's the first time I've ever seen them in our village!"

"You seem pretty excited about that," I said.

"Of course I am!" Frank said. "The tigers use the petals to make their **clubs** stronger. Now we can do the same."

Thea lit up.

"WOW! THIS IS A GREAT SCOOP!"

So my sister grabbed yet another stone **TABLET**. She **quickly** began to chisel the story so we could get the news out fast.

53

"Would you please grant us an **interview**, Professor Flowerfur?" Thea asked.

"Well, actually, I have already given an interview today," he replied. "A rodent in a **pink** outfit came trampling through here before . . ."

We immediately knew who he meant.

"**OH NO, NOO, NOOO!**"
I cried.

A moment later, Sally's voice boomed through the village.

"**NEWS FLASH!**" she cried. "Saber-toothed tigers' secret revealed! A flower as hard as **GRANITE**!"

WAAAAAAAAAH!

Incredible! Sally had beaten us to the story **AGAIN**. The **STONE AGE RATITZER** was going to be awarded in a few hours, and she was the clear favorite to win. Rats!

Heeeelp!

Watch oooout!

Out of the waaaay!

WE WOULD NEVER WIN NOW. WE WERE DOOMED! EXTINCT!

We were about to slink back to the news office when we saw a group of cavemice running toward us.

"GET OUT OF THE WAAAAY!"

"WATCH OOOOUT!"

"MOOOOOVE!"

Gulp!

Squeak!

Grunty and Thea JUMPED to the side of the road just in the nick of time. Hercule and I weren't so lucky. The wave of rodents RAN RIGHT OVER US!

"What's going on?" Thea asked the panicked crowd.

The mice stopped.

"THE ROCKS ARE GROWING!"

"THE ROCKS ARE JUMPING!"

"THE ROCKS ARE HOPPING!"

"Jumping rocks?" Hercule asked. "What are you talking about?"

The rodents started babbling all at once. We couldn't understand a single word they said.

"Bouncing bananas!" cried Hercule. "Calm down and tell us what happened!"

The oldest-looking mouse took a deep breath. "We work in the QUARRY," he explained. "Come there with us and see for yourselves!"

Now, I don't know if you've ever been to the *Old Mouse City* quarry, but it's a vast, rocky area where we cavemice get all our STONE. We use the stone to build our huts and make useful items such as tools and bowls and many other things.

We followed the quarrymice to the quarry, and the old rodent pointed to a cluster of LARGE STONES sticking up higher than others.

"We had just finished our break when the stones began to POP out of the ground," he said. "They were growing like MUSHROOMS!"

"And they weren't just growing," another

They moved!

rodent added. "They were JUMPING, HOPPING, and SWAYING back and forth!"

The rest of the workers nodded.

Thea nodded. "Stones that move! That could be a remarkable **SCOOP**!"

"But they aren't moving now," Hercule pointed out.

"Hmm," I said. "Let's stick around and SEE if they move. Maybe we can finally beat Sally to a story."

So we waited . . . and waited . . . and NOTHING happened.

"Yaaawn. Are you sure you saw them move?" asked Hercule.

"**YES!**" the mice insisted.

Thea sighed. "Bah! There's NO STORY here."

I plopped down on a big rock. "You know what? I'm peeved!" I **snorted**. "I'm hot, my snout is itchy, and there's nothing happening here!"

And at that moment . . .

"WAAAAAAAAAAH!"

Hmph!

"Come on, Geronimo. This is nothing to cry about," Hercule scolded.

"WAAAAAAAAAAAAH!"

"I-I-I'm n-n-not c-c-crying," I stammered, suddenly afraid. I turned as PALE as mozzarella.

Why was I afraid? Because I could feel the boulder underneath me start to move! It slowly pushed up from the ground.

WHAT WAS HAPPENING?

The boulder began to move some more.

PETRIFIED CHEESE! WHAT WAS GOING ON HERE?

Everyone stared in amazement as all the stones suddenly began to jump up and down! I was bounced from one to another like a sack of Paleozoic potatoes.

It was TERRIFYING . . . and PAINFUL!

"HEEEEEEEEELP!"

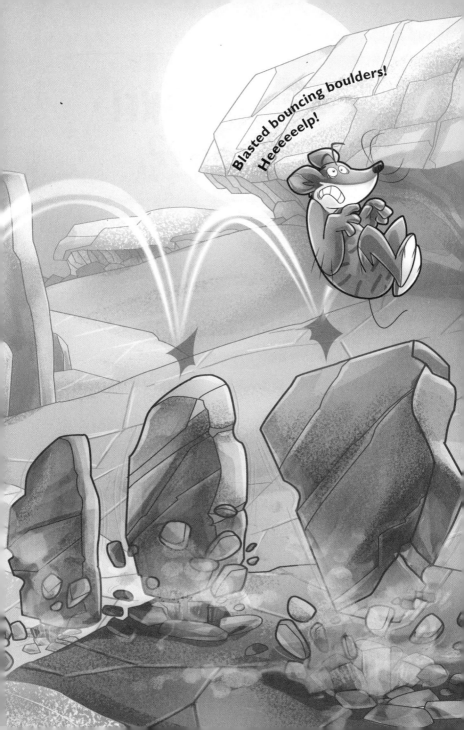

EARTHQUAKE! OR NOT?

One boulder crashed into another boulder, and then all the boulders toppled like **DOMINOES**. The first boulder made the second one fall, the second one made the third one fall . . . and the last one **crashed** into me and made me fall!

BY THE GREAT ZAP! WAS I ABOUT TO GO EXTINCT? I WAS TOO YOUNG TO LOSE MY FUR!

"Geronimo!" Thea yelled.

"I'm here!" I squeaked from under a pile of rocks.

I crawled out from under that pile of debris with dusty fur and **BUMPS** all over my tail. But I was **safe** and **sound**, at least. Of course, that didn't last long.

"You're **lucky** to be alive!" Thea said, looking around happily. She leaned toward me and Hercule and whispered, "The rocks really *do* move. **THIS IS A GREAT SCOOP!**"

"WAAAAAAAAAAH!"

"All right, who keeps crying?" I asked. Hercule had his ear against a pile of loose stones at the end of the cave. "Geronimo! The noise is coming from here!" he exclaimed.

Thea and I **RUSHED** to him and we heard the noise, too. All of us quickly began to push aside the loose rocks. We moved boulder after boulder, slab after slab, and pebble after pebble. At that point the wailing stopped, and the ground began to shake.

BOOOOOOOOOOOOOOom!

Moldy mozzarella! An earthquake! "HEEEEEELP!" I cried.

With my whiskers trembling in fright, I took cover under a big rock. Yes, I admit it; I'm a big scaredy-mouse! But can you blame me? It was an earthquake!

Or was it? When the ground stopped shaking, a creature popped up from the ground. It was a **giant mole**!

Giant moles are large prehistoric creatures that live **underground**. They have powerful **claws** they use to dig long, deep tunnels. Giant moles have weak eyesight and can get disoriented very easily.

NOW I GOT IT!

RUMBLEE

I figured out why this mole was crying. He was lost and couldn't find his way home! The boulders in the quarry must have blocked his underground tunnels. Poor thing — he must have felt TRAPPED, so he dug his way to the surface. Then he really was trapped, until we helped him!

Intrigued, Thea, Hercule, and I slowly approached him. The giant mole might have been big, but he was also **adorable**!

When he sensed us near him, the mole stood up and BURST into a dance.

FOSSILIZED FETA! HE WAS SO HAPPY!

"He must be glad that we dug him out," I guessed.

Thea, on the other paw, looked beaten. I

had never seen her so low.

"So much for our mousetastic **scoop**," she said. "Moving rocks is big news, but a lost giant mole is nothing special. In fact, it's a big, fat f𝐥𝐎𝐩! I'm starting to think that Sally is really going to WIN the Stone Age Ratitzer!"

THE BIG SCOOP

After we showed the giant mole which way to DIG to get out of the quarry, he dove back **underground**. It felt good to help him find his way back home, but we were back to square one. We needed a big **scoop** to beat Gossip Radio! So we said good-bye to the quarrymice and went back to the task of finding some sensational news.

BUT HOW SHOULD WE TRY TO FIND IT NOW?

"We need to clear our heads," I said.

"How about a **nice swim**?" Hercule suggested. "That should reenergize us."

"And we can wash off this quarry dust," Thea added.

As we walked to the river, Grunty started copying my moves, MAKING FUN of me. What an annoying-saurus!

We stopped at a **secluded** place by the river where the current was slow, the bottom was clear, and the water was shallow. The

Hee, hee!

Humph!

perfect spot for a little dip!

I scrambled down the riverbank. I was about to **JUMP** into the water with the agility of a dolphinosaurus when I slipped on a rock and bounced into the river instead!

OOOOUCH!
WHAT A JURASSIC PAIN!

Then I heard a voice behind me. "Geronimo? Geronimo Stiltonoot?"

It was Leo Edistone, the village inventor.

"What are you doing here?" I asked him. He chuckled.

"SEE WITH YOUR OWN EYES!"

While Thea, Hercule, and Grunty *SPLASHED* happily in the water, I followed Leo Edistone to the **LEDGE** of a rock overlooking the river. There I saw a huge tower of boulders with a **strange contraption** sticking out of the water nearby.

"How did you build a tower so tall?" I asked in astonishment.

LEO EDISTONE

Leo smiled. "I did it with my Boulder Builder."

"BOULDER BUILDER?" I asked.

Leo walked over to the contraption and began to turn a crank attached to two **STONE** wheels.

"Thanks to the Boulder Builder, I can lift enormouse **boulders** with little effort," he said.

He turned the **CRANK**, and a boulder

that hung from a pulley overhead began to **rise**.

Then Leo moved a lever, placing the boulder on top of a **TALL** pile of rocks.

"This is just the start," said Leo. "I'm going to build an even **HIGHER** tower.

Then I'll light a FIRE on top of it. That way, anyone using boats on the river at NIGHT can see where they're going!"

That was a brilliant idea! And it was Leo's first really useful invention.

WE FINALLY HAD A MOUSETASTIC NEWS SCOOP!

EXTRA! EXTRA! READ ALL ABOUT IT!

I ran to tell Thea and Hercule. Thea got busy **chiseling** the article. I interviewed Leo Edistone and chiseled a picture of the Boulder Builder. My sister finished writing just as the **sun** was setting. We had to get the story out quickly, before the award was announced!

Thea stayed behind while Hercule and I jumped on Grunty's back and **rushed** to Old Mouse City. Suddenly, I saw Hercule's eyes get very **WIDE**.

"Put your head down, Geronimo!" he ordered.

SWOOOOOOSHHH!

What? Where? Who?

Great rocky boulders, something was flying right over our heads! Whiskers trembling, I looked up and saw a pterodactyl. It was **Zippa**, one of the fire guardians of Old Mouse City.

Every day after **sunset**, Zippa and her partner, Scorch, light the torches in the city that illuminate the streets.

Hercule and I followed the glowing torches to Singing Rock Square. Although the city was LIT UP for the night, we could not see a **SINGLE MOUSE** anywhere! I had to do something to get their attention, so I began to **SCREAM** like a shrieker:

"EXTRA! EXTRA! READ ALL ABOUT IT IN THE STONE GAZETTE! LEO EDISTONE INVENTS SOMETHING USEFUL!"

I repeated this a few times, but not a single rodent came out of their cave. Not one!

"Can't anyone hear me?" I yelled.

"Leave it to me," said Hercule.

He cleared his throat and began to scream like a rat in a trap:

"**Look at this! A huge hunk of Parmesan cheese! Let's not tell anyone else about it!**"

Right away, a wave of rodents spilled into the square. Their noses twitched and their mouths WATERED in anticipation of eating the delicious cheese.

"**Where's the Parmesan?**"

"**Give us the cheese!**"

"CHEESE! CHEESE! CHEESE!"

they all chanted.

BONES AND STONES, WHAT NOW?

There was no cheese!

But Hercule seemed to have the situation
under control.

He stepped in front of the crazed crowd
and pointed to the sky with an innocent
look on his face.

"Up there, look!" he cried. "It's **enormouse** . . . it's **COLOSSAL** . . . it's **MASSIVE**!"

The rodents looked up, but all they could see was the round, full moon.

"But that's the **MOON**!" said Ernest Heftymouse. "Hercule, are you feeling okay?"

"I'm fine! I'm just really excited because . . . because — here!" Hercule cried, snatching *The Stone Gazette* tablet from my paw.

Then he began to shout.

"READ ALL ABOUT IT! LEO EDISTONE HAS FINALLY INVENTED SOMETHING USEFUL! IT WILL HELP ALL CAVEMICE! DETAILS IN THE STONE GAZETTE!"

AND THE WINNER IS . . .

The citizens of Old Mouse City **LOOKED** at one another in amazement.

"Did we hear that right?"

"Something useful?"

"By Leo Edistone?"

That's when **SALLY** showed up. She snatched the tablet and read the article out loud all in one breath. Then she went pale, then purple, and then green — as green as an angry **T. REX**!

"How did I not know about this? This piece of news is *definitely* fake!" she cried out in rage.

"Tsk! Tsk! Look who's talking about fake

news," Hercule remarked.

"Listen up! There's an easy way to settle this," said Ernest. "Let's find **LEO EDISTONE** and see for ourselves!"

Hercule nodded. "Everyone to the river!"

We headed out with a small crowd of rodents marching behind us. When we arrived, we saw that Leo had finished his TOWER and lit a lively FIRE on its top. The village leader was speechless.

"This really *is* useful!" he said.

Leo nodded. "Yes! From now on, the boats traveling

at night will **SEE** perfectly where they're going."

The **CAVEMICE** broke into a thunderous applause. Ernest cleared his throat.

"Seeing the importance of the tower and the fact that Leo Edistone has finally invented something useful . . ." he began. Everyone's ears twitched as they listened carefully while Sally **SIZZLED** with anger.

"I proclaim *The Stone Gazette* and its publisher, Geronimo Stiltonoot, *winner* of the Stone Age Ratitzer!"

The applause got even **louder**, and it was directed at me! Right at me! I became as **red** as a Paleozoic pepper. I can be a rather shy mouse at times.

We all began to celebrate. Some rodents hugged Hercule, who melted like cheese in the summer sun. Grunty started JUMPING up and down happily, and then began to HOP around like a kangaroosaurus. Then, suddenly, Grunty stopped hopping. He scratched his nose, and . . .

"AAAH . . . AAAH . . . AAAAAAACHOOOOO!"

He exploded into the biggest sneeze the Stone Age had ever heard.

What a truly **MEGALITHIC** sneeze it was! It flew through the crowd like a *HURRICANE WIND*, sweeping hats right off the heads of rodents.

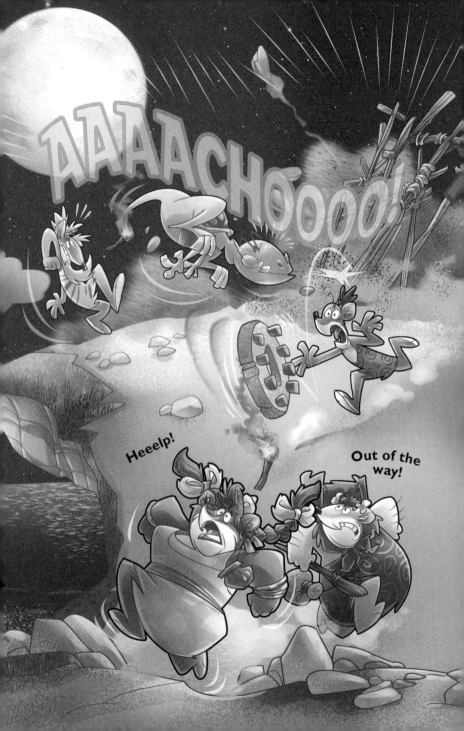

And then Leo Edistone's tower began to **wobble**. Then it began to shake. It shook and shook and shook some more . . . until the boulders began TUMBLING down! We all ran, desperate to not go extinct, as the tower crashed to the ground around us. **BONK!** A boulder hit me on the tail. **BONK!** A rock landed on Hercule's **skull**.

Another rock missed Ernest Heftymouse by a whisker . . . but only because he dove into the river.

Leo Edistone's only useful invention came down with a colossal **crash**. The very last boulder fell right on top of the Boulder Builder! It was **smashed** into a million pieces.

HOLEY BOULDERS! WHAT A MEGALITHIC DISASTER!

When Leo emerged from under a pile of **rubble**, massaging his lumpy head, he said, "I think I have to tweak my invention just a smidge."

"A **smidge**?" I yelled. "I think you'll have to do a ton of work, you useless inventor!"

"Leo, your invention is no invention!" added Ernest. "And that's not a Boulder Builder. It's a bone buster!"

It was also a story buster, as far as I was concerned, because our **big scoop** was now a **big bust**!

"Listen up, citizens of Old Mouse City!" Ernest cried. "Seeing that Leo's invention is not useful at all, Stiltonoot's story is NO GOOD. The Stone Age Ratitzer Award goes to Gossip Radio for its big story about the end of the rainbow!"

Sally Rockmousen's GRIN spread wide across her snout.

"Let's hear some applause!" she called out as four rodents dragged the heavy Ratitzer Award to her. "Give a cheer to the most skilled, brilliant, and ACCURATE JOURNALIST in Old Mouse City: me!"

I rolled my eyes. But then Hercule noticed something in the pile of rubble. "**Well, well, well**. Isn't this the stone that was found at the end of the rainbow?"

NOW WE'VE SEEN EVERYTHING!

FOSSILIZED FETA! HERCULE WAS RIGHT!

There among the fallen **rubble** of stones from Leo's tower was a stone smeared with the **COLORS** of the rainbow. It looked just like the slab discovered by Sally!

"Here's **another** one!" cried Thea.

"There's another one **down** there," said another rodent.

"I see one **up** there!" cried a third.

We were all dumbfounded.

"I can explain," said Leo Edistone. "I found those stones right over there, in that grove."

He pointed to a group of short trees growing on the riverbank. Intrigued, we all walked over to them. Each of the small, SLENDER trees was laden with a **round fruit** I hadn't seen before.

Professor Fred Flowerfur stepped out of the crowd and examined the trees. He began to nod like he was very **impressed**.

"Ooh, these are rare examples of the rainbow tree," said Fred. "And these are its fruits. Look!"

99

Large **multicolored berries** hung from the tree's branches.

"The tree gets its name from the berries," Fred explained. "The juices of the berries are the **COLORS** of the rainbow. The fallen berries must have stained the stones that Leo found."

"Very interesting," said Hercule. "And do the trees grow only **here**, by the riverbank?"

Fred nodded. "Yes."

"And they wouldn't **grow** in the town square?" Hercule asked.

"No, of course not," Fred replied.

"Aha!" said Hercule. He spun around and pointed at Sally. "That means that your 'witnesses' were **LYING**! They did not see the rainbow end in the town square. They picked up one of these **BERRY-STAINED** rocks and brought it there!"

101

The crowd gasped.

"Ridiculous!" fumed Sally. "I am extremely honest! I would never LIE about a story!"

Then I remembered how her witnesses had been HIDING their paws. I saw them skulking behind Sally.

"You there! Show us your PAWS!" I demanded.

"Yes, show us your paws!" the crowd yelled.

Sally glared at the three rodents, but the crowd was too much for them. They held out their paws — which were STAINED with rainbow colors!

The crowd gasped again.

"These so-called witnesses must have dragged the stone to the town square," said Hercule. "It's proof that Sally was lying!"

THE RAINBOW TREE

APPEARANCE: THIN TRUNK
WITH LARGE LEAVES

USES: THE LARGE LEAVES
ARE PERFECT FOR
SHADING A HAMMOCK AND
TAKING A NAP.

FRUIT: LARGE
MULTICOLORED BERRIES.
NOBODY HAS TASTED
THEM YET — VOLUNTEERS
ARE WELCOME!

HABITAT: THE RAINBOW TREE PREFERS A
COOL, WET ENVIRONMENT, LIKE THE BANK OF
A RIVER OR SHORE OF A LAKE.

DREAM: TO PAINT ALL THE GRAY STONES OF
THE WORLD WITH ITS BEAUTIFUL COLORS!

Ernest Heftymouse cleared his throat. "The Ratitzer cannot be given to a fraud. Therefore, the award goes to . . . um . . . FRED FLOWERFUR!"

Puzzled, the crowd just stared at him.

"I mean, um, the AWARD actually goes to, um, the rainbow tree!" Ernest said. "I mean, the rainbow! I mean, um, we're all winners . . ."

"What are you **babbling** about, dear?" interrupted his wife, Chattina Heftymouse.

You must know that Chattina is a rather large rodent, and she can be very, very, very persuasive. She immediately took the matter into her own meaty paws.

"Listen up, everybody!" she called out. "Thanks to the discovery of the rainbow tree, the Stiltonoots have proved that Sally's big news item was fake. The Stone Age

Ratitzer Award, therefore, goes to *The Stone Gazette* for their **scoop** on the rainbow tree and for unmasking Sally as a fraud!"

The cavemice burst into applause.

"BRAAAAAAVO!"

everyone cheered.

Ernest Heftymouse motioned for the AWARD to be brought to me, Thea, and Hercule.

The village leader was pretty confused by now. "Um, congratulations to all the Stiltonoots! Happy birthday! I mean, um, BON VOYAGE! No, wait, I mean, um, happy anniversary!"

BONES AND STONES! HEFTYMOUSE WAS TALKING NONSENSE!

But that didn't matter. Because we had done it! *The Stone Gazette* had finally **won** the Stone Age Ratitzer Award, the most important journalism award in the Stone Age. For real, this time!

And so, after accepting the award, Thea and I lifted it up to celebrate our victory. Actually, we *tried* to lift it up, but it was really **VERY HEAVY**. Humph!

THREE CHEERS FOR GERONIMO!

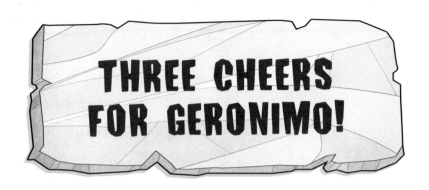

Then the **crowd** picked us up.

"Three cheers for *The Stone Gazette*! **Hip, hip, hooray!**" they all shouted as they threw us in the air.

I closed my eyes in **TERROR** and **FLAILED** my arms as I soared through the air. Thea, instead, hovered with the grace of a prehistoric butterfly. Hercule watched with a smile on his snout, satisfied that he had helped us with his detective skills.

The party continued deep into the night, and when it was over, we were exhausted! We hoped the rodents who had presented us with the Ratitzer Award would carry it for us, but they were sound asleep. So we had to drag it to our office (with some help from Grunty and Leo Edistone).

TRUST ME, IT WAS A COLOSSAL EFFORT!

When we finally got to *The Stone Gazette*, the sun was starting to rise.

We collapsed on the floor, exhausted.

"So much for the Boulder Builder," said Leo, panting. "My next invention will be a Boulder Carrier!"

"Bouncing bananas!" cried Hercule. "Tell me as soon as you've invented it. I'll be the first one to use it!"

But Leo Edistone wasn't listening anymore. He had instantly fallen asleep and

was **snoring** so loudly, we had to leave the office!

As we made our way home, our bones **ached** from exhaustion and our legs felt as mushy as cottage cheese. We YAWNED again and again as we dragged ourselves through the dark streets of Old Mouse City.

We parted at Thea's cave. Hercule waved good night, and I walked over to Grunty. He wasn't the most lovable **DINOSAUR** in the land, but without him and his megalithic sneeze, we wouldn't have uncovered Sally's fraud.

"Thanks, **GRUNTY**," I said. "You've been a big help. I really mean it."

He smiled, and I began to pet him like he was a big, **sweet** puppy.

And then Grunty inhaled so deeply that his face looked like a balloon.

"AAAAAAAH . . .
          AAAAAAAAH . . ."

"No, no, no!" I cried.

"AAAAAACHOOOOO!"

Another sneeze struck me full in the face, messing up my whiskers and almost ripping off my **clothing**! Gross!

And then I felt my nose twitch. Oh no . . .

"AAAACHOOO!" I sneezed.

Petrified provolone! Now I had a **cold**, too! Grunty laughed, and I had the overwhelming urge to turn him into megalithic meatballs. But I was soooo *tired* and starting to feel miserable. So with a runny snout and one **sneeze** after another, I went back to my cave.

Still, I was in a pretty good mood. After all, with all the meteorites, earthquakes,

T. rexes, and saber-toothed tigers, there are far worse problems in the Stone Age than a **cold**!

And that's the scoop, from . . .

AAAACHOOO!

Excuse me. From . . .

Geronimo Stiltonoot, cavemouse!

Don't miss any adventures of the cavemice!

#1 The Stone of Fire

#2 Watch Your Tail!

#3 Help, I'm in Hot Lava!

#4 The Fast and the Frozen

#5 The Great Mouse Race

#6 Don't Wake the Dinosaur!

#7 I'm a Scaredy-Mouse!

#8 Surfing for Secrets

#9 Get the Scoop, Geronimo!

Up Next!

#10 My Autosaurus Will Win!

Be sure to read all my fabumouse adventures!

#1 Lost Treasure of the Emerald Eye

#2 The Curse of the Cheese Pyramid

#3 Cat and Mouse in a Haunted House

#4 I'm Too Fond of My Fur!

#5 Four Mice Deep in the Jungle

#6 Paws Off, Cheddarface!

#7 Red Pizzas for a Blue Count

#8 Attack of the Bandit Cats

#9 A Fabumouse Vacation for Geronimo

#10 All Because of a Cup of Coffee

#11 It's Halloween, You 'Fraidy Mouse!

#12 Merry Christmas, Geronimo!

#13 The Phantom of the Subway

#14 The Temple of the Ruby of Fire

#15 The Mona Mousa Code

#16 A Cheese-Colored Camper

#17 Watch Your Whiskers, Stilton!

#18 Shipwreck on the Pirate Islands

#19 My Name Is Stilton, Geronimo Stilton

#20 Surf's Up, Geronimo!

#21 The Wild, Wild West

#22 The Secret of Cacklefur Castle

A Christmas Tale

#23 Valentine's Day Disaster

#24 Field Trip to Niagara Falls

#25 The Search for Sunken Treasure

#26 The Mummy with No Name

#27 The Christmas Toy Factory

#28 Wedding Crasher

#29 Down and Out Down Under

#30 The Mouse Island Marathon

#31 The Mysterious Cheese Thief

Christmas Catastrophe

#32 Valley of the Giant Skeletons

#33 Geronimo and the Gold Medal Mystery

#34 Geronimo Stilton, Secret Agent

#35 A Very Merry Christmas

#36 Geronimo's Valentine

#37 The Race Across America

#38 A Fabumouse School Adventure

#39 Singing Sensation

#40 The Karate Mouse

#41 Mighty Mount Kilimanjaro

#42 The Peculiar Pumpkin Thief

#43 I'm Not a Supermouse!

#44 The Giant Diamond Robbery

#45 Save the White Whale!

#46 The Haunted Castle

#47 Run for the Hills, Geronimo!

#48 The Mystery in Venice

#49 The Way of the Samurai

#50 This Hotel Is Haunted!

#51 The Enormouse Pearl Heist

#52 Mouse in Space!

#53 Rumble in the Jungle

#54 Get into Gear, Stilton!

#55 The Golden Statue Plot

#56 Flight of the Red Bandit

The Hunt for the Golden Book

#57 The Stinky Cheese Vacation

#58 The Super Chef Contest

#59 Welcome to Moldy Manor

The Hunt for the Curious Cheese

#60 The Treasure of Easter Island

#61 Mouse House Hunter

#62 Mouse Overboard!

Don't miss my journeys through time!

MEET
GERONIMO STILTONIX

He is a spacemouse — the Geronimo Stilton of a parallel universe! He is captain of the spaceship *MouseStar 1*. While flying through the cosmos, he visits distant planets and meets crazy aliens. His adventures are out of this world!

#1 Alien Escape

#2 You're Mine, Captain!

#3 Ice Planet Adventure

#4 The Galactic Goal

#5 Rescue Rebellion

#6 The Underwater Planet

 **Don't miss any of these exciting Thea Sisters adventures!**

Thea Stilton and the
Dragon's Code

Thea Stilton and the
Mountain of Fire

Thea Stilton and the
Ghost of the Shipwreck

Thea Stilton and the
Secret City

Thea Stilton and the
Mystery in Paris

Thea Stilton and the
Cherry Blossom Adventure

Thea Stilton and the
Star Castaways

Thea Stilton: Big Trouble
in the Big Apple

Thea Stilton and the
Ice Treasure

Thea Stilton and the
Secret of the Old Castle

Thea Stilton and the
Blue Scarab Hunt

Thea Stilton and the
Prince's Emerald

Thea Stilton and the Mystery
on the Orient Express

Thea Stilton and the
Dancing Shadows

Thea Stilton and the
Legend of the Fire Flowers

Thea Stilton and the
Spanish Dance Mission

Thea Stilton and the
Journey to the Lion's Den

Thea Stilton and the
Great Tulip Heist

Thea Stilton and the
Chocolate Sabotage

Thea Stilton and the
Missing Myth

Thea Stilton and the
Lost Letters

Thea Stilton and the
Tropical Treasure

Old Mouse City
(MOUSE ISLAND)

GOSSIP RADIO

THE CAVE OF MEMORIES

THE STONE GAZETTE

TRAP'S HOUSE

THE ROTTEN TOOTH TAVERN

LIBERTY ROCK

DINO RIVER

UGH UGH CABIN

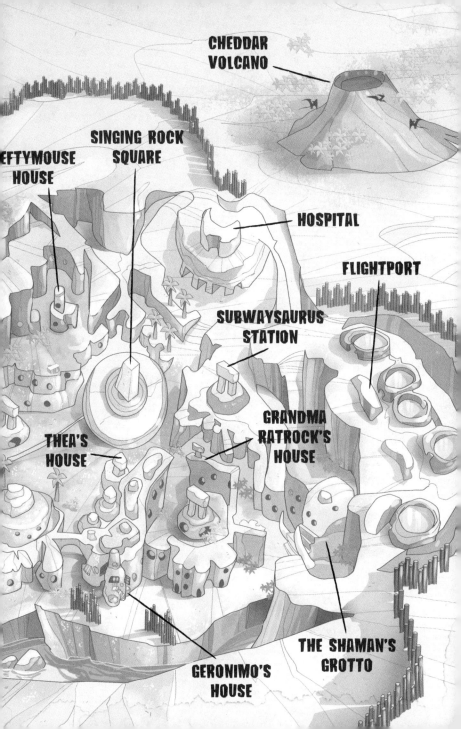

DEAR MOUSE FRIENDS,

THANKS FOR READING,

AND GOOD-BYE UNTIL

THE NEXT BOOK!